The CITY WORM and the COUNTRY WORM

by LINDA HAYWARD
Illustrated by CAROL NICKLAUS

Featuring Jim Henson's Sesame Street Muppets

A SESAME STREET/GOLDEN PRESS BOOK
Published by Western Publishing Company, Inc.
in conjunction with Children's Television Workshop.

"Hey, Slimey!" said Oscar, holding up a thimble filled with water. "You're on."

Oscar meant that it was time for Slimey, his pet worm, to practice his newest trick.

"I can hardly wait to tell everyone about this," said Oscar. "I bet no one has ever seen a worm dive from a diving board into a thimble full of water."

Slimey climbed up the little ladder.

He wriggled to the end of the diving board and looked down. There was the thimble full of water.

Slimey took a deep breath and dived. He landed in the thimble with a SPLISH.

"Terrific dive!" said Oscar. "A few more practice sessions and you'll be ready for the big time."

"Good," said Slimey, as he toweled off. "And now I have to go tidy up my room. My cousin Squirmy is coming to visit me tonight."

"*Tidy* up your room?" cried Oscar. "When my cousin Trashy visits me, I always *mess* up my room."

That evening Squirmy arrived with her suitcase. The first person she saw on Sesame Street was Oscar.

"Excuse me, sir," she said. "I am looking for my cousin Slimey. Does he live around here?"

"Yeah," said Oscar. "Slimey lives right there in that shoebox."

"Thanks," said Squirmy. "By the way, is it always so noisy in the city?"

Oscar looked around at Sesame Street.
Cars and trucks were rumbling by.
The garbage collector was rattling cans.
A police van's siren blared as it sped past.
A rock band was practicing upstairs.
"What noise?" said Oscar. "I don't hear anything.
When you live in the city, you get used to noise."

Just then Slimey wriggled out of his shoebox.
"Cousin Squirmy! How nice of you to come!"
"Cousin Slimey! It's wonderful to be here!"
"Welcome," said Slimey, "to the Big Apple."
"What apple?" asked Squirmy.
   "Oh, that's just a funny name for the big city,"
said Slimey. "We call our city the Big Apple."

Slimey took Squirmy to his room and helped her
unpack.

Squirmy loved Slimey's room. She admired his
plants on the windowsill and his tie-dyed pillows on
the bed and his I LOVE SESAME STREET poster on
the wall.

The next day Slimey gave Squirmy a tour of the city.
He took her to the Earthworm Museum. There
they saw twenty different kinds of dirt in the Soil
Sample Room.
They both enjoyed a colorful mobile entitled "Worm
Turning In Slow Motion."

Slimey and Squirmy ate their lunch at a sidewalk cafe.

That afternoon they climbed to the top of the Sesame Street sign and took in the view.

In the evening they had front row seats at the
biggest earthworm musical stage show in town.
(In fact, it was the only earthworm musical stage
show in town.)

"The city is a very exciting place," said Squirmy,
"even if it is noisy."

The next day it was time for Squirmy to go home.

"Thanks for everything," she told Slimey. "I hope you will come and visit me in the country."

"I've never been to the country," said Slimey. "Do you have a lot of museums and shows and sidewalk cafes?"

"No," said Squirmy. "We have a lot of quiet."

After Squirmy left, Oscar showed Slimey a sign
he had made. "Isn't this a terrific sign?" said Oscar.
"I painted it myself."

"I didn't know that you could dive into a thimble full of water," said Slimey.

"I can't," said Oscar. "You are the diver."

"Then why does your sign say 'starring Oscar T. Grouch'?" asked Slimey.

"Because," said Oscar, "*I* made the sign. Heh heh heh."

"That is unfair," said Slimey. "I think I will go on a long trip. You can do the show without me."

SEE THE AMAZING DIVING TRICK COME TO THE SHOW STARRING OSCAR T. GROUCH

SIZE 10

As Slimey packed his suitcase, he wondered where he should go. Suddenly he thought of his cousin Squirmy.

"I know," he said. "I will visit Squirmy in the country. It will be nice and quiet there — no shows, no signs, no grouches."

Slimey went to the bus stop and waited for the bus.

When Slimey arrived at his cousin's address, all he saw was a big apple lying on the ground. Where was Squirmy's house?

He was very surprised when Squirmy poked her head out of the apple.

"Cousin Slimey! How nice of you to come!"

"Cousin Squirmy! It's wonderful to be here!"

"Welcome," said Squirmy, "to the Big Apple. That's what I call my house."

Squirmy lived in a real apple. Inside the big apple, there was a nice cozy room.

Slimey loved Squirmy's house. He liked the flowers on the table and the patchwork quilt on the bed and the HOME SWEET HOME sampler on the wall.

The next day Squirmy gave Slimey a tour of the countryside. They hiked through the crisp fall leaves. They went for a brisk dip in the local puddle.

They even slept out under the stars.
Slimey had never seen so many stars.
There was only one problem. Slimey couldn't sleep.
It was too quiet.
  "If only Oscar were here," thought Slimey. "He would
make a lot of noise and I could go to sleep."

In the morning Slimey and Squirmy were talking
about this and that when a robin flew up and landed on
the branch of an apple tree.

Was that robin thinking about taking a nap? Was he
planning to sing a song?

Oh, no! That robin was watching Slimey and Squirmy
and he was thinking about only one thing.

BREAKFAST!

"This is the life," Slimey was saying to Squirmy.
"No cars, no trucks, no garbage collectors . . . ."
   Suddenly he looked up and saw a monstrous bird
diving out of the sky, heading straight toward him!
   Slimey was too scared to move. But Squirmy was
not.
   She grabbed Slimey and pulled him into a hole in
the ground. The robin could not reach them.

After the robin flew away, they came out of the hole.
"What was *that*?" cried Slimey.
"Oh, that's just Robin Redbreast," said Squirmy.
"You've seen him before?" said Slimey.
"Oh, yes," answered Squirmy. "You should see all the birds that live around here — robins and thrushes and chickadees. When you live in the country, you get used to birds."

Slimey decided that seeing one bird was enough.
It was time to go home.

"I guess I'm just a city worm," said Slimey, as he
started down the road to the bus stop. "I like living in
the city."

"And I guess I'm just a country worm," said Squirmy.
"I like living in the country."

"Good-bye, Cousin Squirmy! Thanks for everything!"

"Good-bye, Cousin Slimey! Come back soon!"

When Slimey arrived home, he was surprised
to see a sign hanging on Oscar's can. It said:
WELCOME HOME SLIMEY.

The sign made Slimey feel good.

"Well, how's the wandering worm?" said Oscar.

"Tired of riding buses," said Slimey. "But I like
your sign."

"Hey, if you think that sign is great,
wait till you see my new sign for
the show," said Oscar.

And he pulled out another sign.

"Well," said Slimey, "I guess I'd better
start practicing."

ABCDEFGHI